# Give Me Some More Sense

*A COLLECTION OF CARIBBEAN ISLAND FOLK TALES*

*JACINTHA A. LEE*

MACMILLAN
CARIBBEAN

First published 1988 by
MACMILLAN EDUCATION LTD
London and Basingstoke
*Companies and representatives throughout the world*

ISBN 0–333–46121–5

| 17 | 16 | 15 | 14 | 13 | 12 | 11 | 10 | 9 |
|----|----|----|----|----|----|----|----|---|
| 08 | 07 | 06 | 05 | 04 | 03 |    |    |   |

This book is printed on paper suitable for recycling and
made from fully managed and sustained forest sources.

Printed in Malaysia

A catalogue record for this book is available from the
British Library.

# Contents

Foreword                                               v
Acknowledgements                                     vii
Folk tale telling in St Lucia                        viii

Tale of a tail                                         1
The game 'hot'                                         5
Back to the land for Compere Lapin                     9
Burnt behind                                          16
Chicken Land                                          24
Sweet, sweet potato                                   29
Compere Lapin pays a price                            34
Give me some more sense                               39
Mr Turnover                                           44
Compere Lapin and his school                          54

The author                                            67

# Foreword

The publication of *Give Me Some More Sense* is both
significant and timely. This collection of St Lucian folk tales
provides readers with the unique opportunity to appreciate in
printed form some of the many stories which have been orally
transmitted by our older folk generations, and which
consequently form an integral part of our original St Lucian
way of life. *Give Me Some More Sense* appears at a time when
our St Lucian community is being more and more exposed to
foreign values and influences; a time when our true popular
traditions run the real risk of being forgotten or totally
ignored, as we aspire to a way of life which is more modern,
sophisticated and metropolitan in outlook. Gone are the days
of genuine communal living, of working and playing together;
indeed gone are the days when we could so openly confide in
our next door neighbour and share his successes or his failures.
Thus the timeliness of this publication lies in the fact that it
serves to revive our sense of true cultural values and in so
doing serve as a beacon of light which will enable us to
differentiate between what is genuinely St Lucian in our midst
and what passes as 'impoverished entertainment, entailing
impurities of inspiration and extra-cultural influences'. *Give Me
Some More Sense* is indicative of a genuine desire to revive a
neglected and forgotten art form — that of story telling.

The central character of the stories is none other than the
wily and elusive 'Compere Lapin', who invariably prides
himself on his ability to outwit both friend and foe alike. His
varied exploits are related in a style which is simple and direct,

but nonetheless captivating. And indeed this is in keeping with the mode of presentation of the 'raconteur' or story teller as he seeks to make his stories 'come alive' to his listening audience.

The world of *Give Me Some More Sense* is peopled with characters who behave in ways which are singularly typical. It is a world in which action is largely governed by the principle of survival; nevertheless it is a world which, like ours, has its own system of retribution.

It is to this intriguing world that I now invite readers. The stories are meant primarily for the listening ear, rather than the the reading eye, but that should not prevent our enjoyment and appreciation of them. As we read, we should let our imagination wander, so that, after having thoroughly enjoyed *Give Me Some More Sense*, our sense of resolve to salvage the more genuine aspects of our culture from outside infiltration and impoverishment will be immeasurably strengthened.

Jeremy C. Joseph B.A. (U.W.I.)
M. Ed (Bristol University)

# Acknowledgements

This edition of *Give Me Some More Sense* would not have been possible without the help, encouragement and advice of a number of individuals. Special thanks go to Mrs Muriel Gill, Education Officer Curriculum who recognised the need for the inclusion of our own folk stories in the school curriculum. Thanks also to the Anius family, Jeremy Joseph, Joyce Auguste, Louise McVane and Dr Michael Louis for their encouragement and moral support.

Dedicated to Lyndell, Davina, Esther and to the present generation of young St Lucians.

'. . .Let the little children come to me, and do not hinder them, for the kingdom of God belongs to such as these.' *Mark 10:14*

# Folk tale telling in St Lucia

Folk tales or folk stories are told only in patois and are called **Tim-Tim** stories. The term 'folk tales' is used in English to refer to the household tales or fairy tales such as 'Cinderella' or 'Snow White'. It is also legitimately employed in a much broader sense to include all forms of prose narrative, written or oral, which have come to be handed down through the years.

The nature of these stories varies in the different areas of St Lucia and also in the other islands. This probably happened because of the passing of the tales from one island to another.

These tales have their counterpart in other islands as **Anancy** stories. According to Harold Simmons these **Tim-Tim** stories are not indigenous to the West Indies but stem from Africa and the **La Fontaine** fables. They are classified in the great genre of folk tales known as **Animal** tales. Some are designed to instruct and others to entertain.

The stories usually start with the following dialogue between the conteur (teller) and the audience:

**Conteur** Tim-Tim.
**Audience** Bois Chaise.
**Conteur** Qui sa Bon Dieur meté assu Laterre?
**Audience** Toute chose.

'Tim-Tim' and 'Bois Chaise' serve as a theme for the beginning of our stories. 'Qui sa Bon Dieur meté assu Laterre' is translated 'what things God put on earth'. The reply 'toute chose' means 'everything'.

After this introduction, the conteur usually proceeds like this: 'Teni...' (there was once...) or 'un fois' (one day). The conteur then goes on to relate the story.

To conclude the story, some more dialogue follows between the conteur and the audience, which goes as follows:

**Conteur**   E di queek *or* Mesieur.
              E di queek.
**Audience**  Quack.

Most of the stories deal with animals like Lapin (Rabbit), Chat (Cat), Cabuite (Goat), Macack (Monkey), Tigre (Tiger) and many other animals in the animal kingdom. There are also those centring on people, for example a king, a queen, ordinary men, women and children.

These stories, as mentioned earlier on, are not indigenous to the West Indies but stem from Africa. This was possible through the coming of the slaves into the islands. After working in the field for the day, the slaves used to gather in the evening to 'teway leestwaar' (relate stories) as a form of relaxation.

Time is slowly but surely altering the sort of relaxation practised by our ancestors. Though folk tale telling is still predominant in the rural areas of St Lucia, it is unfortunately fast dying out in the city, towns and villages.

*Give Me Some More Sense* is a collection of our own St Lucian folk stories. It tells of the adventures of Compere Lapin, Compere Tigre, Compere Macack, etc.

This collection is aimed primarily at the 8–9 years olds, but it will certainly be interesting reading for older children and adults alike.

## The characters

In Jamaican folk stories the word 'Brer' is placed before the names of the animals, e.g. Brer Rabbit, Brer Anancy, etc. In St Lucian folk stories the word 'Compere' is used, e.g. Compere Lapin, Compere Tigre, etc.

Brief character sketches of those who make up the stories follow.

## KINGS AND QUEENS
The kings and queens as portrayed in these stories do not represent the concept of royalty derived from the European kings and queens.

## COMPERE LAPIN (MR RABBIT)
In reality, rabbits are small in build. In the stories, the rabbit is very much the same size. Though he is the smallest animal, he is the wittiest and most clever. He is able to fool every other animal or individual by his clever schemes. Though some of the other animals may seem to outwit him during the course of the stories, he eventually triumphs over them.

## MADAME LAPIN (MRS RABBIT)
Compere Lapin's wife is as clever as her husband. Following the pattern of human relationships she has to abide by her husband's wishes.

## COMPERE TIGRE (MR TIGER)
Compere Lapin's friend and enemy. At the beginning of each tale or story, Compere Lapin and Compere Tigre are firm friends. But towards the end they become enemies. Compere Tigre is clever, but not clever enough to outwit Compere Lapin.

## MADAME TIGRE (MRS TIGER)
She, unlike Madame Lapin, does not always abide by her husband's wishes. She is a determined character.

## COMPERE CABUITE (MR GOAT) AND COMPERE MACACK (MR MONKEY)
These animals, though clever in their own rights, are not clever enough to surpass Compere Lapin's schemes.

## COMPERE CHIEN (MR DOG)
Compere Chien does not portray the idea of cleverness as in real life. He believes everything which is told to him.

# Tale of a tail

One day, God invited all horned animals to a dinner on the other side of the sea. All the animals wanted to go, especially Compere Chien.

Unfortunately for him, he had no horns.

He walked through the woods trying to work up a plan. He eventually met Compere Lapin. He told Lapin, 'Let we go to the dinner too.'

'But how we go get horns?' Compere Lapin asked.

'I know a place where they make those things, let we go,' Chien told him.

They went to the place and got their horns stuck on. For the rest of the day Compere Chien sat in one place, his head in the air, but Lapin made use of his horns. He went into a garden and started digging out carrots. As a result his horns got lost.

When he returned to where he had left Compere Chien he did not find him. This was because Chien was already on board the boat which was by then far out at sea.

'There is one animal on board who eh got horns,' Compere Lapin shouted.

The Captain hearing this could not believe his ears, so he asked Chien who was closest to him, 'What did the person on ground say?'

Chien replied, 'He eh say nothing.'

Compere Lapin seeing that no attention was paid to him, shouted again, 'You have a dog on board. If you think I lying let all them animals shake their horns.'

Hearing this, the Captain ordered that the boat be stopped. Next, he ordered each animal to shake his horns. Compere Bef shook, Compere Cabuite shook, Compere Mouton shook. All the animals shook their horns except one — Compere Chien.

The Captain told him, 'Shake your horns.'

Compere Chien shook very slowly. He knew that if he shook any faster his horns would come off.

The Captain shouted, 'Shake faster!'

Compere Chien shook so quickly that what he feared happened — his horns popped off, and both he and the horns fell into the sea.

Compere Chien swam until he reached land. He searched the whole day for Lapin. He said to himself, 'I go fix him up, I go fix him up, I go fix him up, that Lapin, when I meet him he going to see.'

After searching for a long time, he was rewarded. He noticed Compere Lapin's tail sticking out from a hole in the ground. Taking hold of Lapin's tail he pulled with so much force that poor Lapin's tail came off, leaving only a very short piece.

This is why, up to this day, all rabbits have extremely short tails.

E di Queek.
Quack.

# The game 'hot'

Compere Lapin sat on his chair and thought,
'I don have nothing to eat in the house today,
what I go do?'

His forever active mind thought of a plan.
Quickly, he started building an oven. When it
was finished, he went down the road whistling.
The first animal he met was Compere Cabuite.

'Compere Cabuite, let we play "hot".'

'What kind of game is that "hot"?' asked
Compere Cabuite.

'Let we go home and you go find out,' was
the reply.

On arrival at his home Compere Lapin said,
'You see the oven over so, man I build it for the
game. I will go inside then you go light it up.
When it hot I will say, "hot" then you go open
the door of the oven, then I go come out and we
go let it get cold, and you go get inside. I will
light it up, and when it hot you have to say,
"hot". After that I go show you the rest of the
game.'

The oven was cold so Compere Lapin went
in while Compere Cabuite lighted the fire.

As soon as Compere Lapin felt a little heat
he shouted, 'Hot.' Cabuite then opened the door.
They allowed the oven to get cold, after which
Lapin lighted it up again.

'Now it is your turn,' he told Compere
Cabuite.

Cabuite entered the oven, and after a while
he shouted, 'Hot.'

'It en hot yet,' Compere Lapin shouted back.

'Yes it hot, wa...a...a...a...a...a...
a......!' Cabuite screamed.

Compere Lapin did not answer but waited
until he heard no sound from the oven which
meant that Compere Cabuite was dead. He then
opened the oven, and said to the dead goat,
'Now it is hot.'

Unknown to Lapin, Compere Macack had
witnessed everything which had taken place.
Every day Compere Lapin did this to a different
animal, until Compere Macack was the only one
around.

At last he approached Compere Macack.
'Macack let we play "hot".'

'I never hear of a game call "hot",' was the reply.

Compere Lapin told him about the game, and then went in the oven. After about one minute he shouted, 'Hot.'

'I sorry Compere, but you too round and too fat for me to let you go without my tongue tasting you,' Macack told him.

On hearing this, Compere Lapin remained very quiet, for the oven was not yet very hot. Macack, who was already very hungry, thought that Lapin was dead and by that time cooked. So he opened the door. Compere Lapin rushed out, knocked out Macack and pushed him in the oven.

Compere Macack shouted and screamed, he pounded on the door, but in vain. When Lapin heard no more sound he opened the door and took out Macack.

'Why you don take your time, you too much in a hurry,' he laughed quietly to the dead monkey.

E di Queek.
Quack.

# Back to the land for Compere Lapin

Compere Lapin looked up at the heavens and shook his head. There had been no food for a long time. The store houses were empty, the trees weren't bearing. If the times did not change, something would have to be done, otherwise people would starve, Lapin thought to himself. The thought of starvation caused Compere Lapin to tremble. Starvation? Not for him!

Compere Lapin sat and thought and thought and thought; what could he do? Every bit of food he had was already gone. He could not ask any of his friends because they were in the same situation as himself.

The thought of going to his land to look for food had never appealed to him. He screwed up his face, rubbed his tummy and stretched, but he still could not come up with any ideas.

'Well one thing for sure,' he told himself, 'I en go sit one place and expect things to come to me. I go get out and look for things, no worms go taste me blood.'

He picked up his cutlass and headed towards his garden. The sun was so hot that Compere Lapin could not even breathe properly. As he walked along he thought, 'They say by the sweat of you brow you go eat bread, well I go sweat so much I go have bread for the rest of me life.'

When Compere Lapin reached his garden he leaned on a tree trunk for a few minutes. He looked at the garden and wanted to go back home but changed his mind. 'Man, nothing to beat a trial but a failure, so I go try. If I fail,' he shrugged his shoulders, 'Well . . .'

Compere Lapin started digging. A few minutes later one of Compere Tigre's children passed by.

'Ah! Ah! Compere Lapin what you doing there?'

'You can see I digging,' he replied still working away.

'But . . . . . . ha! ha! ha!'

Compere Lapin stopped and looked up.

'Let me tell you something, is either you start helping or you just go away.'

Little Tigre laughed. 'Me? Man you mad, I don want to dirty me hands with no dirt.'

'Well go!' Lapin bellowed out.

Tigre ran away laughing. 'Well I never hear more, let me go and give Papa the news.'

Compere Tigre could not believe his ears.

'Lapin is digging up his garden? Ha, ha, ha,

let me go and see for myself.'

Poor Lapin meanwhile was still hard at work. Although he was tired he did not stop. All his energy had drained away, only sheer determination kept him going.

He was still working away when Compere Tigre came by. Tigre could not believe his eyes. He let out a fit of laughter.

'My, my, man what you doing there? Ah! Ah! Compere Lapin you going mad or something. Ha, ha, ha.' Tigre could not control himself, he laughed and laughed and laughed.

Lapin did not bother with him, he kept on digging. He dug until Tigre could no longer see the top of his head.

'Hi there Lapin,' Tigre teased, 'you digging you grave, don be selfish man, make it large enough to hold a lot of us. Ha, ha, ha.'

Tigre hopped away. 'The whole village must hear of that, he go get jokes until he cry.'

Compere Lapin kept digging away. He stopped suddenly. The words 'dig', 'grave', 'large enough to hold a lot of us', flashed in his mind. He scratched his chin and smiled, sweat all over his body.

'I eh selfish man and I go never be selfish. Tigre you don know what you save me from.'

Lapin started working even faster than before. He dug and dug until he had a hole large enough. Being a light and nimble creature he was able to get out of the hole unhurt.

Then he lay under a tree and waited, a broad grin on his face.

After a while he heard footsteps. 'Ah!' he breathed out. Although he was tired he started jumping up and down. His cutlass in the air, he laughed and danced and started singing, 'At last, at last, I eh go starve again, I eh go starve again.' Thinking that Lapin had found some food one of them shouted, 'Compere Lapin, we come to give you a hand but like it is a waste of time. We so hungry.'

'Ah, I know what you thinking,' Lapin smiled. 'I eh so greedy you know, go ahead I left some for you all. It over there.' He pointed to the hole.

On hearing this they rushed past Compere Lapin and dashed towards the hole. Too late they realised that the hole was that deep.

Compere Lapin looked down at them and smiled. 'That will be good meat for days and days, all of you go die after a while.'

Meanwhile those in the hole were frantic; all of them were trying to get out at the same time, but in vain. Each time they tried, more dirt would cave in.

After a while Compere Tigre stopped them.

'Fellas we eh go get out of that hole. Lapin trick us, well he going to pay for it.'

He looked up to see Compere Lapin smiling down at them. He felt so angry that he put out his hand to grab a stone to send after him. He was about to give Lapin what he deserved, when he stopped suddenly. Something was funny about that stone. He took another look at it. He

could not believe his eyes, for he was holding a
potato.

Seeing this, all of them started digging away
wildly. Compere Lapin still kept on smiling.

'Hi there,' he called out, but no one paid any
attention. 'Ho...o...o...oo...o...! How all
you go get out of the hole?'

14

On hearing this they stopped; they had forgotten about that!

'Right,' Lapin nodded, 'I go let you all out if only I get some potatoes.'

'Of course,' was the chorus.

Compere Lapin hopped away and returned with a length of rope. One end he tied to a tree and the other he dropped into the hole. Each one climbed up, took with him a handful of food, half of which went to Compere Lapin.

'Oh!' one of them remarked. 'If Lapin garden have food, mine have too.'

This was echoed by the others who ran away, heading straight to their plot of land.

Compere Lapin sat on his pile of food and shook his head. He could not believe this turn of events.

'Well,' he murmured, 'so we all going back to the land. Well, yes siree.'

E di Queek.
Quack.

# Burnt behind

Compere Lapin and Compere Tigre were in the habit of stealing eggs belonging to the Queen. Neither knew that the other was a thief.

The Queen, noticing the continual disappearance of her property, decided to set a trap for the thieves. She instructed the guards to place a tar-baby, a human-shaped object covered with tar, to sit in the garden.

A few hours later, Compere Lapin went in search of his usual meal of eggs. When he entered the place the first thing he saw was the tar-baby. He crept up slowly to the dummy and asked politely, 'What is your name? I just come to see the nice eggs.'

On receiving no reply, he repeated his question, but in a much louder tone. Still no reply. By this time Compere Lapin was really getting mad; how dare this black fella ignore him like that!

'O...o...o...o...is that, is style you have so. You not answering me. Well take that.'

He gave the tar-baby a nice solid slap across the face. His hand got stuck.

'Let me go, man let me go. Ah! Ah! Man I eh joking you know.'

Another slap, the next hand got stuck. Lapin pushed and pulled. As a result he got his knees stuck on as well. He struggled and struggled but in vain.

Then along came his dear friend Compere Tigre. 'What is wrong with you? Man, what the matter?'

Compere Lapin bawled out, 'Shut up man.'

Compere Tigre was dumbfounded. He just could not understand what his friend was up to. Lapin meanwhile was trying to figure out how he could trap Tigre.

'You know that I married,' he began.

'Yes.'

'You know I have a wife,' he continued.

Compere Tigre was growing impatient. 'Sure man, sure I know that stupid chick you have.'

'Would you like a wife?'

'Sure man, sure,' Tigre replied hastily, but on second thoughts changed his mind. 'No, no, no thank you, sir. I eh want one.'

'Man not me wife I giving you, man come closer.' Tigre crept up to him.

'The Queen say that the person she find stick on this thing would have to marry her daughter. Man you believe a small ugly animal like me can ever marry the Queen daughter? A fella like you would suit her just right.'

Compere Tigre could not believe his ears. He leaned back on his heels and smiled.

'What news, marry the Queen daughter? You right, you not nice enough.'

With these words he pulled out Lapin and stuck himself neatly on to the tar-baby.

'Phew! Man, thanks a lot you don know what you save me from. Don forget to invite me to the fete.'

'That all right man,' Tigre told him laughingly. 'You know I would always help you out. You can move on.'

When Lapin left, Tigre laughed. 'Invitation? An ugly thing like him?'

Compere Tigre waited impatiently. He kept

frowning and sucking his teeth.

'Where this Queen? Is time I get organise with a beautiful wife.'

He started smiling as he heard footsteps behind him. He looked up to see the Queen standing a few feet away.

'Good morning m'am, I hope your daughter is as beautiful as your Majesty.'

'As . . . . . . as . . . . . . how dare you!' the Queen screamed at him.

Compere Tigre looked at her in amazement.

'Oh, if your daughter is like you, I think I will change me mind about marrying her, I sorry.'

'What are you talking about, marrying my daughter? I have no daughter, so stop talking rubbish.'

'Guards!' she called out. 'Prepare the hot irons.'

'Hot irons? But Your Majesty, I thought that you said you had no daughter, and you preparing the hot irons to press my suit for me.'

'Suit? Suit? I will press something much better than you suit, your nice fat . . . . . . '

She tapped his buttocks.

At last Tigre really understood what was going on. The realisation that he was in for something hot and painful dawned on him.

'Your Majesty, Your Majesty, please let me go.'

The Queen did not even look at him but called out, 'Guards! Guards! Quick get the piece of iron.'

At this point Tigre could hold the strain no longer.

He started crying. 'Wa...a...a...a...a ...aaa...a...please My Majesty, My Majesty, have mercy on me.'

'Get a bag and put him in it,' she ordered.

Tigre was put into a bag, after which the hot iron was placed on his buttocks, and removed after a short while. Tigre screamed and screamed and screamed.

'Untie him.'

Compere Tigre came out of the bag sniffing and rubbing his eyes. He quickly dragged himself away crying out, 'Lapin will pay for this, he go pay for it. When I catch him I go do him worse than what they do me. Wa...a...aaaa...a... a...a...a,' he screamed as a small stone landed on his burnt behind. He looked around frowning but he saw no one.

Suddenly he heard someone singing.

'Tigre, Tigre, burn bam-bam.
Tigre, Tigre, burn bam-bam.
Tigre, Tigre, burn bam-bam.'

'I know who you is,' Tigre said in a timid voice. 'When I hold you, you will see. Yes, Lapin you fool me and you go pay for it.'

'How much,' the voice called out after a burst of laughter.

'Yes, yes, you can laugh, after joy come sorrow.'

With these words he headed for home.

Tigre kept on brooding over his misfortune. Day after day he kept on looking for Compere Lapin. During one of his outings he came upon a figure, which seemed to him to be covered with worms.

'Ah! Ah! who are you, and why you have all dem worms on you, what a mess, go clean yourself up.'

'Clean myself up? Nothing go clean me up. I try everything.'

'Bu...bu...bu...bu...who do you this?' Tigre asked.

'I was passing by Compere Lapin home. When he see me he clear his throat and spit on me. This is why I have all these worms on me.'

Tigre looked around with a scared expression, 'I eh believe you. Ah! Ah! How Lapin can do that?'

'How Lapin can do that? Well go at his home and you will see. After he do me that, he told me to go and show myself to you. He say he waiting for you.'

Compere Tigre opened his eyes wide, and started to tremble.

'Waiting f...f...f...f......ff...for me?

Well go tell him he go never find me. You know what I go do? I will go home and cover myself with a mattress. Then he go spit all his spit, but he eh go find me to spit on, no siree, not me Tigre. Let me get out of here.'

Tigre ran away as fast as he could.

Meanwhile the figure was murmuring.

'Let me get all them pieces of paper off me body, he! he!'

The costume was hastily removed to reveal Compere Lapin!

E di Queek.
Quack.

# Chicken Land

Compere Lapin and Compere Tigre were sometimes friends and sometimes enemies. This came about because Compere Tigre had always wished to eat up Lapin.

One day Compere Tigre was preparing dinner at his home. He had a big roasted chicken on his table. At that same time Compere Lapin came to pay him a visit. He looked through the keyhole to see what was going on inside. He noticed the roasted chicken and longed to eat it.

He knocked at the door, then quickly looked through the keyhole again to see Tigre's actions. He saw Tigre trying to open the drawer of the table as fast as he could, and placing the chicken in it. Compere Tigre then rushed to the door, rubbing his eyes as though he had been asleep.

'How are you?' asked Tigre in a weary and yawnish voice.

'I all right. What about you, you okay?' asked Lapin, scratching his chin.

'Come in, come in, sorry you late for supper.'

'Don worry about that,' Compere Lapin said meekly as he sat near to the spot where he knew that the chicken was hidden.

Compere Tigre went and lay down on his bed thinking that everything would be all right.

Lapin started speaking, 'One time I gone overseas you know,' at the same time opening the drawer.

'What country you check out?' asked Tigre, sounding bored.

'Man I check out Chicken Land,' replied Lapin while he got hold of the chicken.

'You make money there?'

'Ah! Ah! Man what you saying? Chicken Land full of parts you know,' replied Lapin while he got hold of the chicken's head. 'The first part I gone to was Heady.'

'The people had like you in Heady?'

'Yes, man, the scene was all right, but I check out of there and I gone down to Necky. Man if I tell you about Necky you go pass out. I move to another part, Wingy.'

'Wingy had anything to talk about?'

'Wingy was a bit all right, but I just don dig that place so I move to a place call Body. Ah! boy, look a place great! Man there eh have nothing to prevent you from doing what you like.'

'What about gold and them things. You get any there?'

Compere Tigre started getting a bit tired of this tale.

'No, no I speak about food. I leave there and went down to Thighy, that place was loaded with food. I cool off there for a while and gone lower to a village called Leggy. I find I was wasting my time so I quit the place and came back here.'

'What happen, you not going abroad again?' yawned out Tigre.

'Ah! Ah! It so late, what! How time could fly so? Yes, I see you sleepy and all so I go head for home, sleep tight,' and off Lapin went.

As soon as Compere Tigre shut the door, Lapin started to run as fast as he could.

Tigre went to the table to enjoy his roast, but was in for a shock, for only bones reminded him of his chicken.

'We...l...l...l...ll...l, so all the time he talking about Chicken Land is my chicken he was enjoying.'

Three days passed with Compere Tigre still longing for revenge. He pretended to have been sick and suddenly died. He then sent a young Tigre to Compere Lapin's home to tell him the news. When the young Tigre arrived at Lapin's house he knocked at the door. 'Any body there?'

'Who there?'

'Papa Tigre was sick and he die so I come to let you know because I know you all good friends.'

On hearing of his friend's death, Compere Lapin quickly made the sign of the cross, and shook his head slowly. They set out for Compere Tigre's home. Lapin followed the Tigre, breathing heavily and muttering, 'My God, how terrible.'

He really felt sorry for Tigre, sorry for all the tricks he had played on him. He was so grieved he did not suspect a thing. On arrival at Tigre's home, the young Tigre opened the door and went in. Lapin hesitated at the door.

'Are you sure he dead?'

'Yes.'

Compere Tigre, meanwhile, was straining his ears to hear the conversation.

'He sneeze before he die?' asked Lapin in a whisper.

'No.'

'Ah! Ah! You eh know before somebody die they must sneeze.'

On hearing this, Tigre let out one great big sneeze.

Compere Lapin made one rush out of the door and shouted, 'I too smart for you Compere, you eh go catch me. You eh know when

somebody dead he don sneeze? Ha! ha! ha!
. . . . . . '

E di Queek.
Quack.

# Sweet, sweet potato

Compere Lapin and Compere Tigre were
very good friends. Compere Tigre always ate at
Compere Lapin's home, but Lapin never had the
chance to eat at his friend's home.

One day, about lunch time, Compere Tigre
arrived at Lapin's home.

'Phew!' he exclaimed, sounding very worn
out. He had a bag of potatoes in his hand. He
informed his friend, 'I just leave my garden,
man, I tried and I hungry like joke.'

'I got some cook potatoes but the gravy eh
cook yet, so if you wait a while I. . .' Compere
Lapin didn't have time to finish what he was
about to say for Compere Tigre interrupted.

'Man if I wait one second again I will faint.'

'Okay, okay.'

Compere Lapin gave Tigre a pot full of
cooked potatoes, instructing him to take a few.
Leaving the pot with Compere Tigre, he went to
the kitchen to see whether the gravy was already
cooked. On his return to the room where Tigre

was, he noticed that there were two potatoes left in the pot. Compere Lapin did not protest, but ate what was left. After a short while, Tigre left with his bag of potatoes. He did not have the courtesy to offer some to his friend.

Next day Compere Lapin went to pay his friend a visit. He timed himself so that he would arrive in time for lunch, which in fact he did. Compere Tigre was angry, but he did not show his friend that he was. He detested sharing his food with anyone.

'Wha happening Compere?' sang Lapin. 'How
things your side?'

'I there trying,' Tigre forced a smile. He was
silently praying for Compere Lapin to go away.
Lapin did no such thing, but pulled up a chair
and sat down.

'I know what I will do,' Compere Tigre
thought. 'He go leave in a minute.'

'Listen man,' he called out. 'My belly full, I
think I go leave this food for tomorrow
morning.'

He thought this would send Lapin on his way. He was in for a shock for Compere Lapin said, 'I eh hungry myself you know, but I eh feeling too well now so I think I go catch a sleep by you.'

Compere Tigre, realising that Lapin had no intention of leaving, and feeling hungry all of a sudden, said, 'I think I go eat.' He uncovered the pot of potatoes and extracted all the biggest ones, which he placed in the oven. 'These eh cook,' he informed Compere Lapin. 'What is that again, all my biggest potatoes don cook.'

'Don cook?' But Lapin was not fooled. He was familiar with Tigre's tricks and greed.

'Is like you eh go get from what that good you know,' Tigre continued.

'That all right,' Lapin told him. 'I know you a man of good heart.'

'What you mean, of course I always good to you,' said Tigre frowning at the turn of the conversation.

Compere Lapin went to stand by the oven and said, 'Compere, I see you eh have pigs, but I have a lot. Since all those potatoes eh cook properly I think I go have them for my pigs.'

Compere Tigre saw it was no use to argue. After Lapin's departure, Tigre started to cry.

'Compere Lapin took all me potatoes. I greedy, I greedy, that why that happen to me.'

Compere Lapin meanwhile was enjoying these big well-cooked potatoes.

'He! he! Tigre really greedy, I hope he learn a lesson.'

E di Queek.
Quack.

# Compere Lapin pays a price

Compere Lapin could not stand gossip. He always got really annoyed any time he came across a group of animals discussing other people's affairs.

'But what wrong with them, they only talking about other people.'

Compere Lapin tried telling them that this was a bad habit to indulge in, but they only teased him.

Compere Lapin started getting really angry. He decided to ask God a favour.

'Mr God, these animals really talk a lot you know, teach them a lesson. Any time they talk about anyone let them fall unconscious for one hour.'

God granted him that favour. Next day Compere Lapin filled a basket with all kinds of plants and seeds. There were yams, lettuce, cabbage, potatoes, dasheen and many others. These he started planting on a piece of hard dry rock, singing away as he worked.

A few minutes later Compere Tigre passed by, he could not believe his eyes. What was Compere Lapin doing on this dry place!

'Compere Lapin,' he called out. 'Man what you doing there?'

'Well Compere, I just planting a bit of food. You know how hard things are these days,' Lapin sang out, but still working away.

Compere Tigre scratched his chin and moved away.

'You mean to tell me on this rock Lapin go plant food? The man must be going ma...a... aa...a...'

Compere Lapin smiled as Compere Tigre fell unconscious to the ground.

'Ah!' he breathed out. 'That one that go mind his business later on.'

He then placed Compere Tigre under the naked sun.

'One whole hour of this go make him regret he said that about me.'

Compere sat under the shade of a tree and waited until the hour was up. Tigre got up frowning. He could not understand what he was doing there. His eyes were sore, his lips were dry, some of the hair on his body had even got burnt. Tigre rubbed his eyes and looked at Lapin.

'Compere, what happen to me?'

'Well, Compere, that was a lesson on

minding you business.'

'Bu...bu...bu...bu,' Compere Tigre stammered.

'If you tell the others why you in this state, the same thing go happen to you again,' Compere warned him.

'Okay Compere, I eh go tell nobody,' Compere Tigre said as he limped away.

Compere Lapin smiled and looked around to see whether there was a new victim in sight. He saw no one, not even Compere Pigeon who sat on the tree above him. Pigeon had seen everything that had taken place!

Every day a different animal suffered the same fate as Compere Tigre. They could not warn the others for fear of a repeat. After a few days, Compere Pigeon decided to make his appearance. He placed a towel over his back and passed near Lapin. He said nothing except, 'Good morning Compere,' and continued on his way.

Compere Lapin stopped and frowned. 'That funny,' he said to himself.

'Compere Pigeon,' he called out, 'I there working hard. I planting something here so that I go get some food later on.'

'Work away, Compere. I myself going for a bath and a trim. See you Compere.' Pigeon walked daintily away. Compere Lapin could not believe his eyes and ears, he shook his head slowly.

'Ah! Ah! Pigeon really fresh you know. You mean to tell me Pigeon have hair on that bald head of his for him to trim? His head looking like a...a...a...a...a...'

Compere Lapin could not understand why the trees were dancing around him, why the ground was getting closer, closer, closer and closer.

Compere Pigeon, a little distance off, smiled as he saw Compere Lapin fall to the ground. He ran to the spot and said to the unconscious Lapin, 'Do unto others as you want them to do to you, Compere.'

E di Queek.
Quack.

# Give me some more sense

Compere Lapin, afraid that he might lose his position as the smartest creature around, decided to ask God for some more sense.

God told him that if he really wanted more, he should be able to do three things.

'What are they?' asked Compere Lapin.

'The first thing I want you to find out for me,' God said, 'are the names of the seven people living in that brick house over there.'

It was a very big house built without windows or doors, so that it was impossible for Compere Lapin to find out the names of the people living there.

Anyway he started thinking of a plan which would help him. So, much to the amazement of his friends, Lapin started eating up dead frogs, as many as he could find. Next, he went to the brick house and started piercing a hole through the wall. Then he placed his buttocks to the hole, and released something which caused great confusion in the room. Putting his ear to the hole, he was able to hear every word spoken.

'You are really nasty, Monday, for doing such a thing without asking to be excused,' a voice said.

'Not me, it was Tuesday.'

'Oh, how dare you, it was Wednesday.'

'How can you tell such lies, it must be Thursday.'

'It is not me, it is Friday.'

'That's not true, it is definitely Saturday.'

'Oh, oh! please don't say that, it must be Sunday.'

So through the commotion Compere Lapin learnt the names of the occupants of the house. Feeling pleased with himself he approached God.

'Mister God,' he began, 'I know the names of the people. They are Sunday, Monday, Tuesday, Wednesday, Thursday, Friday, Saturday.'

'Well, well!' God exlaimed. 'The second thing I want you to do is to bring me a quart of wild cow's milk.'

Compere Lapin immediately set off, a bottle in his hand, in search of the milk. He walked a few miles before he spotted a wild cow coming. Thereupon, Lapin started to speak in two tones of voice saying aloud to himself, 'Yes she can, no she cannot. Yes she can, no she cannot.' He repeated these phrases until the cow came abreast with him.

'What are you saying?' asked the cow.

'Oh,' replied Compere Lapin, 'a little negro boy was just arguing with me. He said that you don have milk to fill this bottle.' He indicated the bottle in his hand.

The stupid cow gave him the bottle full of milk and said, 'Go and show the stupid negro the milk.'

Then off ran Compere Lapin, the bottle in his hand to show to God. 'You are very good indeed,' God congratulated him. 'The last thing I want you to bring me is a wild pig's tooth.'

Compere Lapin set off with a piece of iron. After a while he spied a wild pig approaching. At once he started conversing in the different tones as before saying, 'Yes he can, no he cannot, yes he can, no he cannot.'

'What are you saying?' asked the pig in a very big voice.

'I met a stupid little boy down there. He wanted to fight and make big trouble with me, because I told him that you can break this stone.' He indicated the iron.

'That's nothing impossible to do,' replied the pig. He took the iron from Compere Lapin and started to bite, but the 'stone' wouldn't even crack. He gave it yet another bite, as a result one of his teeth came off. Compere Lapin picked up the tooth eagerly and quickly ran to where God was waiting.

'There you are, Mister God. Now for my sense,' said Lapin, smiling broadly.

He patted his tummy, heaved up his shoulders and said quietly to himself, 'Ah! Now I shall be bursting with sense, sense for days and extra days.'

'Lie down under the calabash bowl which is under this tree,' God told him, 'and I will give you sense.'

· Compere Lapin did not do as he was told, but put a frog there instead. Suddenly there was a flash of lightning and a blast of thunder, which caused the calabash bowl to break into bits, thereby killing the frog.

'You thought you could fool me,' Lapin shouted. 'You wanted me to die.'

'Don't you want any more sense?' God asked softly. Compere Lapin remained silent.

E di Queek.
Quack.

# Mr Turnover

One day, Compere Lapin set out to the river to do a bit of fishing. On arrival at the place, he searched until he found the spot where he usually did his fishing. He always caught a number of fishes there because no one but himself knew of this spot.

This private place was a hole hidden from view by a large stone. Any time he went to the river to fish, Compere Lapin would roll away the stone, push in his hands and pull out a number of fishes.

That day, as usual, Lapin pushed in his hand. He got the shock of his life which caused him to scream in pain. Something had got hold of his hand!

'Let me go, plea......se,' he pleaded. He looked all around him and stamped his feet impatiently.

'Ah! Ah! Let me go, who you think you is to hold me so.'

Suddenly a gruff voice came from the hole.

'I will let you go, but whatever I tell you to say, you must repeat.'

'Yes, yes, yes.'

'Good, now I want you to say, "If you are Mr Turnover, turn me over." Only then I will set you free.'

Lapin, anxious to be released, shouted, 'If you are Mr Turnover, turn me over!'

As soon as Lapin said these words, he felt himself thrown high up in the air. Poor Lapin then landed hard on his back about fifty yards from the spot.

Compere Lapin rubbed his back, stretched and hurriedly looked around. He did not see Compere Macack high on a tree looking down at him. Neither did he know that Macack had seen everything that had taken place.

Much to Compere Macack's amazement, he saw Lapin go back to the same hole and push in his hand. Exactly the same thing happened. He landed at exactly the same spot as before. Macack could not understand why Compere Lapin was playing such a dangerous game.

Next, he saw Lapin searching through the bushes until he came up with some pieces of iron. Lapin started sharpening the ends. Still Macack could not understand Compere Lapin's game. That done Lapin planted the iron, the sharp points upwards, at exactly the same spot where he had been thrown. Then and only then, Compere Macack understood what Compere Lapin was up to.

Although Compere Macack was not loved by the other animals, he decided to warn them of Compere Lapin's trick. The first he met was Cabuite.

'Compere, let me tell you something.'

'Talk, nice boy,' Compere Cabuite teased him.

'Well, Compere Lapin go tell you he have a place full of fish...'

'Fish? Fish? Man you mad. There eh have no kind of fish these days,' Cabuite laughed out.

'Listen to me. If Lapin ask you to go to fish with him don go.'

'Don go? Man move your ugly face by me. You don know how long I eh eat fish?'

'Please, please, listen, don go because he go kill you.'

'Look here, Compere Macack.' Cabuite started getting annoyed. 'Move by me, I believe you want all them fishes for your self.'

'That not true, please don......'

Cabuite could not stand Macack any longer, he had never liked him because of his ugliness. He was so annoyed that he fired a kick after poor Macack who barely escaped.

Compere Macack tried warning the others but he came up against hostility every time. He was teased, beaten and spat upon. Poor Macack could do nothing else but go back to his usual hiding place.

Next day, Compere Lapin returned accompanied by Compere Cabuite. 'You know how hard it is to get fish these days, but I never ran out. Because you my friend, I go show you where I catch all my big fish,' he told Cabuite.

He pointed to the hole. 'This is the place. You fish here and if you catch any fish you go have to give me some. I go fish over there.'

Compere Cabuite hastily pushed in his hands, a grin on his face. The grin disappeared immediately his hands were in the hole.

'Wa...a...a...a...La...a... pin,' he screamed.

Compere Lapin rushed to him. 'What happen to you?'

'I...I...I..., something hold my hands.'

'Something hold you hands? Don worry, I sure is fish. When I was small I use to hear the old people say that when a fish hold you, you have to say something, if you don say it, the fish do eat up all your hands.'

'T...t...t...t...ttt...el me wh...wha... what to say.'

'Okay say, "If you are Mr Turnover, turn me over".'

Compere Cabuite breathed out heavily. 'If you are Mr Turnover please, please, please turn me over.'

What Lapin had planned for happened. Compere Cabuite was thrown high up in the air and landed right on the pieces of iron. Poor Cabuite died instantly.

Compere Lapin ran to the spot, pulled out the dead Cabuite and said with a broad smile on his face, 'I go eat curry Cabuite tonight.'

Compere Macack saw what had happened and shook his head. 'I warn him but he eh believe me.'

Every day, Lapin did this to a different animal, until Macack could stand no more. He decided it was time to teach Lapin a lesson. Next day, he climbed down from his hideout and went for a walk knowing he would eventually meet up with Compere Lapin. As usual, Lapin was on the lookout for victims. He met up with Macack.

'Ah!' he thought. 'Look another stupid one, good, that one go be easy.'

'Morning,' he sang. 'I going fishing, you want to come? I know you go come, because you eh eat fish for days.'

'Okay.'

'That good. Know something? You the only one I showing my secret fishing place. Don tell anybody.'

'I go keep my mouth shut,' Macack murmured.

On arriving at the spot, Compere Lapin told Compere Macack, 'Fish here, behind this stone. I go fish over there.'

'No, I prefer to fish over there,' Macack told him.

'Wha happen you don want fish? I showing you a place where you go get a lot of fish, you saying no?'

'Well, if there have a lot of fish, why you eh go and fish there yourself?' Macack said.

Compere Lapin realised that Macack would not fall for that, so he said, 'Okay, okay I go fish there, go another place.'

Compere Lapin pushed in his hand, just at the front of the hole. After a short while he shouted, 'Compere Macack, Compere Macack, I catch a big fish. Come help me pull it out.'

Compere Macack went over and stood there looking at him. He knew what Lapin was up to.

'Come on man, help me pull out this fish.'

Lapin pleaded, struggling as though he had really caught a fish. He smiled as Compere Macack slid his hand, but he got a nasty shock, for the unexpected happened. Macack pushed Lapin's hands further into the hole.

Compere Lapin opened his eyes wide, beads of sweat broke all over his body, for Mr Turnover had got hold of him.

'Hi there Compere, I...I...I...I stick, I stick, the fi...fi...ish hold me.'

'Well Compere,' Macack sang out. 'When I was small, the old people use to say, when a fish hold you, and you want it to let you go, you must say, if you are Mr Turnover, turn me over.'

Compere Lapin's eyes grew wider, he was really frightened. He screamed and screamed and screamed.

'Compere Lapin, you don want the thing to let you go?'

'Yes, yes.'

'Well say the thing I tell you to say.'

'Wha...wha...wha...wha...it...it... a...a...a...gain?'

'If you are Mr Turnover turn me over,' Macack sang out.

Lapin could not understand where Macack had heard of this phrase. Anyway he started, 'If, if, if, if...'

'Come on Compere Lapin, say it,' Macack urged.

'If you, you, you,' Lapin stammered.

'Say it,' Macack screamed.

'Compere Macack,' Lapin told him, 'the words cannot come out. I think I know why. There is some thing over there that is stopping the words from coming out of my mouth. Go over there you go see some pieces of iron, pull them out and bring them here.'

Macack went over to the spot. After his departure, Lapin smiled.

'Good, Macack tink he smart, I go teach him a lesson. When this thing let me go he go find out.'

A few minutes later, Compere Macack came

back carrying the pieces of iron.

'Good,' Lapin beamed at him. 'I believe I go say it now.'

He smiled and said sweetly, 'If you are Mr Turnover, turn me over.'

Lapin kept on smiling as he was thrown through the air, but he was in for a most frightening shock, for in place of the pieces of iron were three sharply pointed pieces of stick.

'God, I sorry for all the things I do already,' he cried as he made his descent.

E di Queek.
Quack.

# Compere Lapin and his school

By Robert and Jacintha Lee

**Characters in the play**
Compere Lapin,
Compere Tigre,
Madame Lapin,
Madame Tigre,
Compere Cabuite, Chien, Mouton, etc. and their children.

*Scene one*

**Conteur**   Messieurs, queek. Compere Lapin decided one day to build a school in order to teach his friends' children. So, one afternoon, he call a meeting of all the animals to tell them about his school. (*Animals enter, singly, and in groups, and talk animatedly until the entrance of Compere Lapin.*)

**C. Lapin**   My dear friends, I wish to welcome you here. I hope that you will all co-co-co-rate with me. As I told you in my letters

54

and the last meeting we had, my school will be of great benefit to the community and indeed to the world as a whole. I will be filled with gratitude and encouragement if you agree to send your talented, intelligent, well-fed, healthy children to my school starting tomorrow, seven o'clock sharp.

C. **Tigre**  Oui Compere, I will bring toute, in fact I have a dozen.
*(Other voices of assent)*

C. **Lapin**  That is good, but you must all remember that on no account must you visit the children at school. Because, if the children see you all, they will cry and will not be able to study their work.

C. **Chien**  I have fourteen children. I don't mind not seeing them for a few days. And furthermore, the way things hard today, they better study hard and not be looking out the window to see when I coming for them, because one day I won't be there, and they will be here. So Compere Lapin, I don't mind, you keep them in the school and beat them if they don't learn, especially the second girl, she too anafer, and as for . . .

C. **Lapin**  Okay, okay, okay, Compere Chien. That is very good. I will do my best for you and for all the parents of this great little community.

(*Other animals promise to bring their children.*)

**C. Lapin**  Sa bon, I want you to know that I preciate you, my friends. Don't be afraid to bring all your children tomorrow. Madame Lapin will be only too pleased to take care of them. (*As the animals move off*) By the way don't forget to give the children all they need, because six months away from home will be a long time.

**M. Tigre**  Not see my children for six. . .

**C. Tigre**  Ah shut up, famme. Compere Lapin, you do what is best.

**C. Chien**  With fourteen children, you think I mind. And if I tell you what my third boy do this morning. . .

**C. Lapin**  Bye, bye. I will see you all tomorrow.

*END OF SCENE ONE*

*Scene two*

**Conteur**   So Messieurs, Compere Lapin and
Madame Lapin open their school the next
day. Bright and early, all the parents start
arriving at the school house, bringing their
children behind them. Compere Lapin
looking like a real schoolmaster, talk soft
to the parents and pat the children on
their head. You could already hear the
people saying that they better send up
Compere Lapin to represent them in the
House of Assembly, he looking like a real
diplomat.

**C. Lapin**   (*to a group of parents in patois*) Eh
bien, you understand. It is after six months
have passed you will see your children.
Understand.

**Parents**   Oui, Compere.

**Conteur**   So the parents bringing their children
and then they going away. After everybody
go, Compere Lapin put the children to sit
on the floor and begin to talk to them.

**C. Lapin**   Now children, today you come to
school to learn (*A child cries*). No children
must cry in my school. And furthermore,
we will start doing work from today, from
now.

**Children**   Yes, Teacha.

**C. Lapin**   Now listen carefully. I will read out the problems to you.

**Children**   Yes, Teacha.
(*Somebody in the back begins to fight. Cries.*)

**C. Lapin**   Shut up your mouth, you hear what I say? Behave yourself. You all have no home training.

**Children**   Yes, Teacha.

**C. Lapin**   Okay. Now I will read the sum.
(*Opens a book and holds it upside down.*)
The sum is, how much blood do you have in your fingers. Now start to work out the answer.

**Children**   Yes, Teacha.

**C. Lapin**   Very good, children.

**Children**   Yes, Teacha.

**C. Lapin**   Oh shut up.

**Children**   Yes, Teacha.
(*A little boy starts to misbehave. C. Lapin glares at him but he does not stop.*)

**C. Lapin**   Mr Zabeau!

**Child**   Oui, Teacha Compere Lapin?

**C. Lapin**   Stand up and say 'Sir'.

**Child**   Oui, Teacha Compere Lapin Sir.

**C. Lapin**   Look at me Mr Zabeau. Your father sent you here to learn not to misbehave. (*Lapin holds him by the neck.*) Is bad for the children, you will only spoil other people children.

**Child**   Oui, Teacha Compere Lapin.

**C. Lapin**   Sir! say 'Sir'! (*He gives Zabeau a knock on the head, Zabeau falls to the floor, children start to scream.*) Shut up, ti cooyons, he is only sick. I will call my wife to nurse him. Madame Lapin, Madame Lapin.

**M. Lapin**   (*Running in breathless.*) Yes doo-doo.

**Children**   (*Pointing to Zabeau on the floor.*) Take him to the sick-room. (*To children*) Come on, do some work, when you all leave here I want you all to have a lot of brains. So start counting each others' fingers. Hurry. When I come back I want to see everybody busy. Now I and the madame will bring Zabeau to the sickroom. I don't want to hear no noise.

**Children**   Yes Teacha Compere Lapin. (*C. Lapin is about to open his mouth to remind them when they all say*) Sir.

*(C. Lapin and his wife drag Zabeau behind the screen separating 'sickroom' from class room.)*

**M. Lapin**   (*Licking her lips*) Is good meat. All tigres taste doux.

**C. Lapin**   Shh! No so loud, the children will hear you. I have to go now and give them some more work to do.
*(Goes back to children, who are still in the process of counting the amount of blood in each others' fingers.)*

**C. Lapin**   Children listen. Now children it is time to go to bed.

**Children**   Ah! Ah! to sleep?

**C. Lapin**   Paix la! to sleep I say.
*(Children lie on the floor to sleep. Suddenly a sound is heard outside. Lapin looks frightened. Runs to his wife.)*

**C. Lapin**   Tigre and his wife are coming. (*Runs back to children.*) Wake up, wake up, let us do some work.

**Children**   But Teacha, we just start to sleep.

**C. Lapin**   Well it is time you get up. Let us do some work. All of you will now say: Seck, seck, glo seck. Seck, seck glo seck.
*(Children repeat)* Yes, yes, this is very good.

Now children you can all go to the other room to play. (*Children leave.*)

**C. Tigre**   (*Entering*) Yes, Compere, you is a very good teacha.

**C. Lapin**   Thank you. When you see my students leave my school they are going to be so intelligent they will be able to make books.

**M. Tigre**   Yes, our Compere is a very good teacha. But there is one thing I cannot understand. I did not hear my son Zabeau. He have a very big voice and I did not hear him. I want to see my children.

**C. Lapin**   Shh. You will disturb the children in the other room.

**M. Tigre**   I don care. I want to see my children.

**C. Lapin**   Compere, will you take your wife away from here? Please take her away. Women always like to cause trouble.

**M. Tigre**   I will not go away unless I see my children.

**C. Lapin**   Okay, okay, come back in three weeks, and I will let you see your children. If you still keep on making this noise, I afraid I will not allow you to see your children.

**M. Tigre**   All right, I agree, but. . .

**C. Tigre**   But but what. You don hear what the teacha tell you?

**M. Tigre**   Quittez moi bat misere moi. I will go, but when I come back I will demand to see my children. You understand me? Ou comprend moi?

**C. Lapin**   Yes, I understand you. And now, will you please go, I cannot tolerate such women in my house, is bad for the children to hear such noise.

**M. Tigre**   (*Screaming*) Let me tell you some...

**C. Lapin**   Compere, take your wife away. Ah! Ah! this lady mad or what.

**C. Tigre**   (*Going up to his wife who has taken hold of Lapin's throat and grabs her by the hand.*) Let us go.
(*They exit.*)

**C. Lapin**   Eh bien, well, well, well, sa se lavie. Women! Women! Women! Children, come here to sleep. (*Children come in. Three start to misbehave.*) I have already said that I do not want children to start to misbehave in my school. Look at what happen to Zabeau, he is still sick. (*Children still misbehaving.*) These children still misbehaving, you all will go to the sickroom, for my wife to cure you all of this disease. Come on. (*He takes*

*them out to the sickroom, comes back.*)
Children, why don't you all be sick, eh? I
know you hate working. If you are all sick
you will do no work. So anytime you want
to go to the sickroom, just say 'sick',
understand?

**Children**   Ah! Ah! play sick.

**C. Lapin**   Yes, play sick, there will be no school
while you all sick. As soon as you want to
go out, just say 'sick'.

**Children**   Sick.

**C. Lapin**   All of you all sick one time. The
nurse will not be able to attend to all of you
at the same time. Anyway half of you will
go now. I will tell you which to go. I want
the fattest boys, so that the nurse will be
able to operate on them nicely. Now I will
pick out the ones to go: you, you, you. (*As
he points, children run off.*) Now the rest of
you better start saying your prayers. All of
you had better kneel down.
(*Children kneel.*)

**M. Lapin**   (*Entering*) Compere, I tie all the rest
already. You sending those now?

**C. Lapin**   Finish already? Go to the sickroom
with my wife.

**Child**  But Teacha, Compere Lapin Sir, we was praying.

**C. Lapin**  I say go to the sickroom now! (*Children run off.*)

**C. Lapin**  After you do these we will pack them all in a box and go away.

**M. Lapin**  Okay. (*Exits*)
(*C. Lapin sits on the floor. After a while, M. Lapin enters.*)

**M. Lapin**  Compere come and help me pack them in the box.

**C. Lapin**  Okay, okay.

*END OF SCENE TWO*

*Scene three*

**Conteur**   So Compere Lapin and his madame
    packed up all the children in two big boxes.
    They were very pleased that their little trick
    had worked. They would have enough meat
    to eat for a long, long time.

**C. Lapin**   (*Trying to pack some of the children
    in a box, but they keep hopping out. Lapin is
    furious.*) What is wrong with you all? Stay
    inside the box. (*But they keep climbing out.*)

**M. Lapin**   (*Shouting*) What happen, you cannot
    control them? Children, get into this box
    now. (*Children all jump into the box.*) Hurry
    Lapin, Tigre and the others might come
    soon.

**C. Lapin**   Yes, let us. . . (*Stops, hearing noise.*)
    Did you hear that, Madame, they are here!
    They are here! (*Runs towards his wife. They
    cling to each other.*) What will we do?

**M. Lapin**   What will we do? Run away of
    course. You want Tigre and Chien to eat us
    up?

**C. Lapin**   Yes, I mean no. Let us get out of here
    fast. (*Both exit.*)

**Children**   (*Jump out of box and start dancing
    and singing.*) Lapin put his tail between his

legs and run away. (*Repeat twice.*)
(*Tigre, Chien and the other parents enter.*)

**C. Tigre**   Yes, our Lapin is a very good teacha,
very good teacha.

**All (Children and Parents)**   Lapin put his tail
between his legs and run away. (*Repeat.*)
*All exit (still singing.)*

*THE END*

# The author

*Photographer: McNeil Jn. Marie*

Jacintha Anius Lee was born at Laborie, St Lucia. She is a qualified teacher, holds a Bachelor of Education Degree and a Diploma in Mass Communications. She worked for several years in St Lucia as an Audio Visual Aids Officer attached to the Ministry of Education and Culture. She presently lectures in Educational Psychology at the Sir Arthur Lewis Community College, St Lucia.